KU-201-404

First published in Great Britain in 2001.
This edition published in 2006 by Brimax Publishing Ltd
Appledram Barns, Birdham Road, Chichester, PO20 7EQ, UK
© Brimax Publishing Ltd

All rights reserved.
No part of this publication may be reproduced, stored in a retrieval system,
or transmitted in any form or by any means electronic, mechanical, photocopying, recording or otherwise
without the prior written permission of Brimax Publishing Ltd.

Printed in China

Rory's Story

BRIMAX

Rory the tiger is having a terrible time!
He has a new baby sister.
She is very small and cries a lot, and
she waves little, clenched paws in the air.
Rory does not know what to think of her.
She is too small to play with him.
He is afraid to hold her in case she slips.
Now his mother and father are always busy.

"Will you cuddle me?" asks Rory.
"In a minute," says Mother Tiger.
"First I have to feed the baby."
Rory waits . . .
"Will you cuddle me now?" asks Rory.
"Soon," says Mother Tiger.
"First I have to wash the baby's ears."
Rory waits . . .

"Will you give me a ride on your back?"
asks Rory.
"Soon," says Mother Tiger.
"First I have to wash the baby's face."
Rory waits . . .
"Will you give me a ride on your
back now?" asks Rory.
"Soon," says Mother Tiger.
"First I have to wash the baby's tail."
Rory sighs and goes to see if his father
will play with him.

"Will you climb a tree with me?"
Rory asks Father Tiger.
"Soon," says Father Tiger.
"First I have to finish straightening
up the den." Rory waits . . .

"Will you climb a tree now?"
asks Rory.
"Soon," says Father Tiger. "First I have
to teach the baby how to growl.
Do you want to help?"
"No," says Rory, feeling a little bit
left out, and sad, and bored.
Everyone is so busy.

Rory goes outside. Hippo comes
bouncing along the path.
"Hi!" says Hippo.
"Do you want to play a game?"
"Okay," says Rory, grinning.
"What should we play?"

Crocodiles!

They have a fun game!

First Hippo pretends
to be a crocodile
chasing Rory.

Then Rory pretends
to be a crocodile
chasing Hippo.

The two friends run in circles until they fall over,
laughing and kicking their legs in the air.
They pretend to SNAP! big crocodile teeth.
SNIP SNAP! Growwwl!

Mother Tiger opens the door,
looking angry.
"Ssshh, you two!" she says.
"You are making too much noise.
You will wake the baby . . .
There, she is crying already."

Mother Tiger goes back inside.
Rory and Hippo hear
the little cub crying, but after
a while the sound stops.

"Let's take a look," says Hippo,
"I haven't seen your new baby sister yet."
So they tiptoe inside.
Mother Tiger is holding the baby
and singing softly to her.

"Hush, little tiger, don't growl and cry,
Mama's going to sing you a lullaby.
The jungle is green, the sky is blue,
Your brother Rory wants to cuddle you."

"No, I don't!" says Rory.
"I don't know how."
"It's easy," says Mother Tiger.
"Sit down and I'll show you."
Mother Tiger brings the baby over to Rory.
Suddenly, there is Rory's new baby sister,
all cuddled up on his lap.
She feels warm and soft. She smiles.
Rory smiles back.

"You're nice," says Rory.
His baby sister makes a gurgly growl back.
She clasps his paw tight. Then she closes her
eyes and falls asleep. Mother Tiger puts the
baby back into her snug corner of the den.

Rory and Hippo creep back outside
to play a quiet game.
"She's okay, my baby sister,"
says Rory to Hippo.
"She's cute," says Hippo.
"You're lucky, Rory."

Now Rory tells everyone in the jungle
about his new baby sister.
"She's soft and warm!" he says.
"She can clench her fists!" he smiles.
"And she's got a gurgly growl," he grins.
Then he practices his own lullaby
to sing to his little sister.

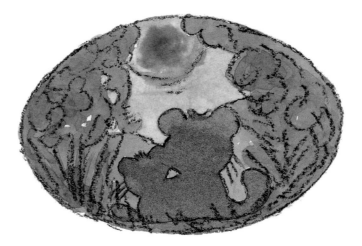

"Hush little sister, don't cry at all,
Rory will hold you so you won't fall.
The jungle is green, the sky is blue,
Your brother Rory is proud of you."

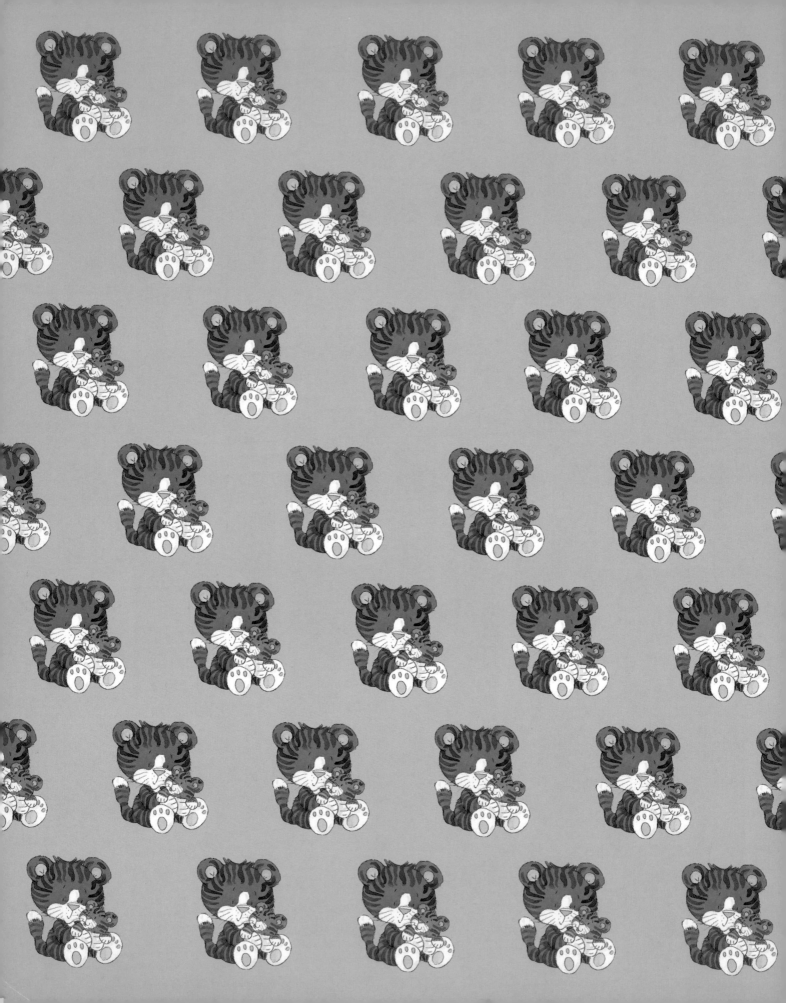

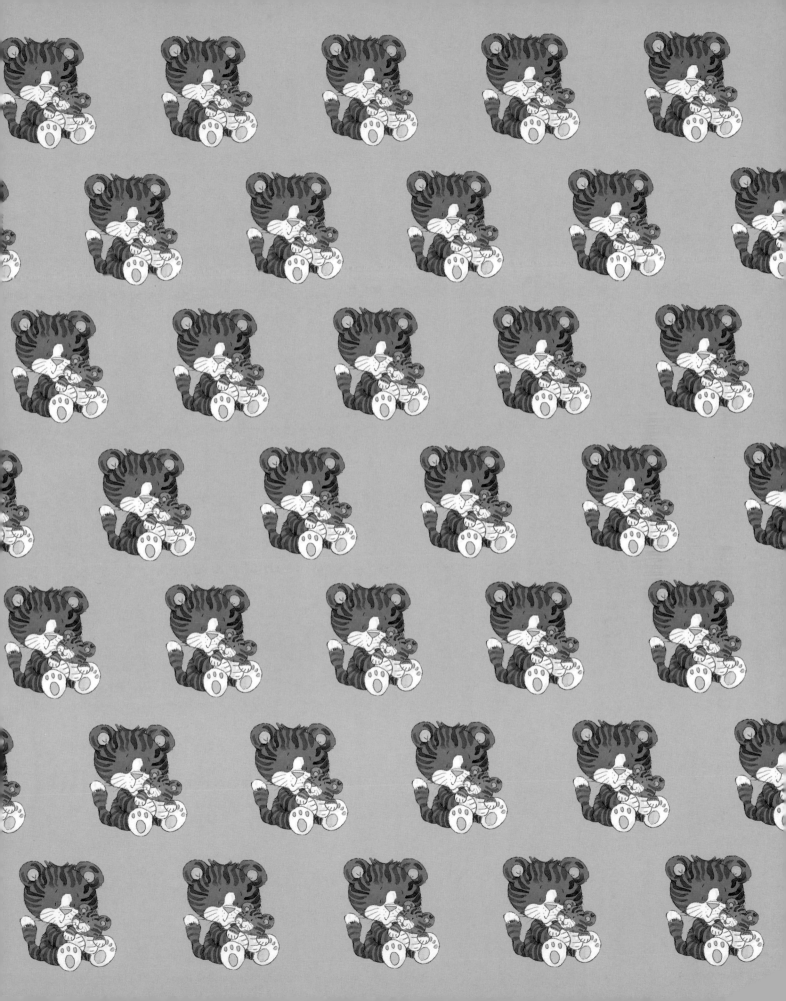